Cookie McCorkle
AND THE CASE OF THE
Crooked Key

SHARON CADWALLADER

Illustrated by Patrick Chapin

AN AVON  CAM

Because the level of maturity and dexterity varies from child to child, adult guidance and close supervision are strongly recommended on the recipes at the end of this book. No child should ever attempt to use kitchen appliances or cooking utensils without first securing permission from an adult.

COOKIE McCORKLE AND THE CASE OF THE CROOKED KEY is an original publication of Avon Books. This work has never before appeared in book form.

AVON BOOKS
A division of
The Hearst Corporation
1350 Avenue of the Americas
New York, New York 10019

Copyright © 1993 by Sharon Cadwallader
Illustrations copyright © 1993 by Avon Books
Interior illustrations by Patrick Chapin
Published by arrangement with the author
Library of Congress Catalog Card Number: 92-97473
ISBN: 0-380-76896-8
RL: 3.0

First Avon Camelot Printing: July 1993

CAMELOT TRADEMARK REG. U.S. PAT. OFF. AND IN OTHER COUNTRIES, MARCA REGIS-TRADA, HECHO EN U.S.A.

Printed in the U.S.A.

OPM   10   9   8   7   6   5   4   3   2   1

A Trip to Bluff Bay

"Cookie, would you describe the inside of that private jet again?" Robert Chin looked eagerly at his friends, Cookie McCorkle and Walter Sousa. They were all sitting on the front steps of their apartment building.

Cookie rolled her eyes slightly at Walter, then cleared her throat. "Well, like I told you before, there was a nice section with sofas and chairs just for lounging—then on the other side of the cabin was. . . ."

"Yoo-hoo, Cookie, Walter! Please come upstairs. I want to talk to you."

The children looked up to see Mrs. McCorkle leaning out the window above them. The McCorkles' apartment was on the third floor. Right next door was where Walter lived with his mother.

"Okay, Mom," Cookie called back. She picked up Moriarty, her wirehaired terrier. "Come on, Walter. See you later, Robert."

Walter followed Cookie into the apartment building. As Moriarty's ears began to flatten slightly in fear of the elevator, Walter reached over and patted his head.

"What do you think your Mom wants?"

"I don't know," Cookie replied, "but I'm glad I got out of describing the plane one more time to Robert."

"Well, you know how Robert is," Walter said. "He's crazy about anything mechanical or electronic."

Cookie nodded. "At least he's not going on and on about our not getting a bunch of money for solving 'The Case of the King's Ghost.' Maybe he's finally catching on to the fact that I'm in this detective business for the challenge, not for the money. All I ever want is a souvenir of a case when it's solved."

"Me, too," Walter agreed firmly.

Cookie had started her detective agency early in the summer and already she and Walter had solved four important cases. She was hoping to crack a few more before school started in the fall.

"Maybe Miss Allgood had to go to the hospital?" Walter suggested as he and Cookie stepped out of the elevator and headed for the McCorkles' apartment.

Miss Allgood, Walter's babysitter, had been home in bed for several days with a bad cold. Meanwhile, Walter had been staying at the McCorkles. He was there most of the time, anyway.

"Walter, people don't go to the hospital with a cold," Cookie said sharply.

"Maybe she has pneumonia," Walter said.

"I doubt it."

When they walked inside the McCorkles' apartment, Cookie's mother was sitting on the sofa. She motioned for Cookie and Walter to sit down.

"I want to talk to you children," she said again.

Cookie looked over at Walter and shrugged, then dropped Moriarty on the rug and sat down. Walter sat down next to her.

"Cookie," Mrs. McCorkle began, "you remember my cousin, Nancy Merrit?"

Cookie nodded. "Yes, she's the one who visited us two years ago."

"That's right," Mrs. McCorkle responded. "Well, Nancy just telephoned to say she needs my bookkeeping skills to help her with her new business."

Mrs. McCorkle was a bookkeeper and

kept an office in the back of the apartment. She worked most of the day. This left Cookie a lot of time to solve detective cases—and to cook, which was her second favorite pastime. Cookie looked at her mother now, wondering why she was telling them all this.

"You see, several months ago Nancy inherited an old mansion in a small town up the coast," Mrs. McCorkle continued. "She's turning it into a bed-and-breakfast inn."

"A what?" Walter asked.

"A kind of hotel, Walter," Cookie explained. "People convert old houses into places where you can spend the night in a real bedroom and then have breakfast in the morning . . . you know, real cozy."

"Nancy plans to open her place in a month or so," Mrs. McCorkle went on. "And she wants me to come up there for a week or so and set up her bookkeeping system on her new computer."

"That's okay, Mom," Cookie said. "Walter and I can take care of ourselves . . . and Dad's home at night."

Mrs. McCorkle shook her head. "No, Cookie, Nancy invited you and Walter to drive up with me. She says Bluff Bay is a lively little town and you children will enjoy

4

exploring the area. I already called Walter's mother. She said it was a fine idea since Miss Allgood isn't much better and won't be back to work for at least a week."

Cookie frowned. "But there's not much crime in small towns."

Mrs. McCorkle smiled. "Well, you've only been back from Hawaii for a few days, Cookie. I think you are entitled to a little rest."

"Yeah, Cookie," Walter agreed. "You said yourself that Sherlock Holmes had to take a rest now and then from his cases."

Sherlock Holmes, the famed English detective, was Cookie's idol.

"But what about Dad?" Cookie said, changing the subject. "He can't cook. He'll miss us."

"We won't be gone that long," Mrs. McCorkle replied. "He can eat at Wang's Restaurant and bring home pizzas. He'll be fine."

"He can eat with my Mom," Walter suggested, but when Mrs. McCorkle and Cookie stared at him, he lifted his shoulders in a defeated gesture.

"Just an idea," he said.

Mrs. Sousa worked in a department store and was always too tired to cook when she came home in the evening. She was in the habit of bringing takeout food from a nearby deli to pop in the microwave. Walter usually tried to eat with the McCorkles.

"We won't be gone long," Cookie's mother assured her. "I'll have to get back to my regular accounts. It will be a short trip—probably a week, ten days at the most."

Cookie sighed, but Walter was delighted.

"When do we leave?" he asked.

"Tomorrow morning," Mrs. McCorkle announced. "Now I must get back to my office. Are you planning to make dinner tonight, Cookie?"

Cookie nodded. "I think I'll make porcupine meatballs," she said. "I thawed some ground turkey and ground beef this morning."

"That will be lovely," Mrs. McCorkle said as she headed down the hall. In a minute Cookie and Walter could hear her office door click shut.

"Oh boy!" Walter exclaimed happily. "Another vacation. First Greenwood Lodge, then Hawaii, now Bluff Bay. What a summer!"

Cookie was silent, then she let out a groan.

"Remember Sherlock Holmes and his need for a rest," Walter reminded her quickly.

"Yes, Walter. I remember. But Sherlock Holmes didn't have to start school in the fall." She sighed and rose from the chair. "Come on, let's start dinner. I want to bake some potatoes and that's going to take an hour or so."

In the kitchen, Cookie took the meat out of the refrigerator while Walter went into the pantry to get the potatoes.

"I'll scrub them really good," Walter said as he put the potatoes in the sink and reached to get the little brush that was hanging on a hook.

"And don't forget to prick them with a fork," Cookie added.

"I won't," Walter replied.

Cookie and Walter worked silently. When Walter was finished fixing the potatoes, he put them in the oven which Cookie had turned on earlier. Then he watched Cookie as she added the rice to the meat.

"Look at the way rice cooks in those meatballs," Walter exclaimed. "It's like magic."

Cookie smiled. Walter was the biggest fan of her cooking. In fact, that was one of the reasons she had made him the assistant in her detective business. Also, she thought Walter had quite good hunches for an eight

year old. At ten, Cookie had learned that hunches were often as important as clues in difficult detective cases.

"What are you going to fix with the meatballs and potatoes?" Walter asked.

"I haven't decided," Cookie said. "We should have some kind of vegetable rather than just a green salad. My Dad may not get fresh vegetables for a while. He's rather absentminded in his eating habits, you know."

"Well, how about coleslaw with your special dressing?" Walter suggested. "Cabbage is a good vegetable."

"Good idea, Walter. Would you get out the cabbage and wash it?"

When Mr. McCorkle arrived home from work, the potatoes were baking, the meatballs were simmering, and Walter was shredding cabbage while Cookie mixed up the dressing.

"Ah, the fragrant aroma of Chéz McCorkle," Mr. McCorkle said in a fake French accent. Then he kissed his fingers and flung them toward the ceiling. Walter grinned, but Cookie just shook her head. Her father's imitations and jokes were usually very corny. But Walter loved them.

"How's tricks, kids?" Mr. McCorkle asked

and flipped Walter's baseball hat around so the bill was in the front again. He had given Walter his old high-school team hat and Walter was never without it.

"We're going to visit Mom's cousin, Nancy," Cookie said, without much enthusiasm.

"I know, your mother called me at work," Mr. McCorkle said. "But you don't sound too excited about the trip."

"Cookie's afraid there won't be any cases to solve in Bluff Bay," Walter explained, as he dumped the shredded cabbage in a bowl.

"Ah-ha," Mr. McCorkle said. "I understand how you feel, Cookie, but you never know. Remember Greenwood Lodge."

Cookie perked up slightly, thinking about the mountain resort and how she and Walter had solved "The Case of the Polka-Dot Safecracker."

"Turn on the news, please, Dad," Cookie said. "Let's see what's happening in the city."

Mr. McCorkle snapped on the television to Cookie's favorite news channel and turned it up so she could hear it in the kitchen.

The newscaster was saying: *"Well, viewers, today was a very quiet day in the city.*

No robberies or murders, only a couple of minor car accidents. It's been a very pleasant day."

The boring news made Cookie feel a little more cheerful. At least, she wouldn't be passing up some fascinating crime here at home.

A few minutes later, Mrs. McCorkle came out from her office and began to help Walter set the table.

"You know, Cookie," Mrs. McCorkle said as she folded the napkins under the forks, "I just remembered something Nancy said about the McKenna Mansion—that's the name of the place she inherited. She said there was something strange about the house—a mystery that had never been solved."

Walter's eyes widened. "Is it haunted?"

Mrs. McCorkle shook her head. "I don't know, Walter. Nancy just said there was something about a mysterious death in the house back in the last century."

Mrs. McCorkle turned and left the kitchen, carrying a cup of coffee for her husband into the living room.

"Did you hear that, Cookie?" Walter said eagerly. "An unsolved mystery!"

"Yes, I heard, Walter," Cookie said. "It's

not a crime that's going on now, but it might be worth investigating."

"Maybe it will be our next case, Cookie," Walter persisted.

Cookie looked up from mixing the coleslaw. "Maybe, Walter, maybe," she said quietly.

The McKenna Mansion Mystery

"So this is Bluff Bay?" Mrs. McCorkle said, half to herself, as they stared down at the little town below them.

"And this is the bluff," Walter added, looking around.

Cookie, Walter, Moriarty, and Mrs. McCorkle were stopped at a look-out point on the highway and were gazing out the window of the car. A few hundred feet below them lay a neatly arranged town set on a small bay.

"Looks pretty dull to me," Cookie said with a frown.

"I think it looks nice," Walter said quickly. "A person could walk from one end of the town to the other in just a few minutes."

"That's what I'm afraid of," Cookie said. "It's *too* small."

"Don't jump to conclusions, Cookie," Mrs. McCorkle said cheerfully. "Let's drive down and find the McKenna Mansion. I think I remember Nancy's directions."

Within ten minutes, Mrs. McCorkle pulled up in front of a large white house on a large corner lot. It was trimmed in yellow, and a newly painted picket fence circled the yard. The landscaping looked as if it needed a good gardener.

"It's a lovely Victorian-style house," Mrs. McCorkle remarked. "Not like some of those back in the city."

"It's Queen Anne style," Cookie remarked casually.

Walter looked at her in surprise. "How do you know that?"

"By all the fancy wood patterning. I read this book on Victorian houses last year."

"Wow, Cookie, you know everything," Walter said with admiration.

"The new paint is quite nice," Mrs. McCorkle said. "I think it will be a very appealing bed-and-breakfast. Let's go see if we can find Nancy."

They all got out of the car, including Moriarty, who was restless from being cooped up so long. He ran happily in circles until

Walter picked him up and carried him through the front gate.

A comfortable porch circled the house and Cookie had to admit it was a pretty nice place. Before they could knock on the door, it opened and a dark-haired woman stood smiling at them.

"Welcome to the McKenna Mansion," Nancy said, giving Mrs. McCorkle and Cookie a hug. Then she shook Walter's hand.

"I'm glad you could come, too, Walter," Nancy said, smiling.

The trio, with Walter still holding Moriarty, followed Nancy into a large entry room with recently refinished wood floors and handsome dark furniture. Several doors led off the entryway in different directions.

"All the furniture was here when I arrived," Nancy explained. "My uncle started to restore the place before he died."

"How fortunate that he was able to get it started for you," Mrs. McCorkle said.

"Yes," Nancy continued. "And in the attic I found bedding and beautiful linen tablecloths and curtains. All I'm really having to do is modernize the electricity, add a few bathrooms, and do some painting."

Cookie looked through a couple of the doors that were slightly ajar. One room looked like an old-fashioned parlor. Through the other door she could see bookshelves, making the room look as if it were some kind of library.

"We'd like to know about the mystery," Walter said suddenly. "Cookie's a detective, you know."

Nancy smiled. "Yes, I understand she's solved several cases already this summer. Unfortunately, there's not too much to the McKenna Mansion mystery, but I'll tell you what I know."

As they walked around the first floor of the house, Nancy explained the history of the McKenna Mansion.

"The house was built in 1885 by a sea captain named Elijah McKenna. I guess he was planning to get married, although he was almost sixty years old then. Sure enough, several years later he brought a young wife to the house and they lived here with Captain McKenna's elderly sister. Hardly anyone in the town ever saw them, though, and they became known as recluses. Then one day there was a small fire in the house and young Mrs. McKenna suffocated. It wasn't too long after that that Captain McKenna and his sister boarded up the house and moved away."

"Where did they move?" Cookie asked quickly.

Nancy shrugged. "No one knows. The house stayed empty for years. When Captain McKenna died it was passed down to a distant cousin, and then to his son who was my uncle. No one seems to know very much about the McKenna family. I even checked the local library to see if there was anything in the newspapers about Mrs. McKenna's death, but I found nothing to add to what I already knew."

"So your uncle and his father never lived in the house very long?" Cookie asked.

"No," replied Nancy. "They had businesses elsewhere and the house was too much to use as a summer home. I'm surprised they didn't sell it."

"Maybe because it's haunted," Walter suggested, his eyes growing wide at the thought.

Nancy smiled. "Some of the townspeople say that before I came there were occasional noises from the house during the night, and that when cars passed by you could see lights in the windows, but I think it's all imagination. The electricity isn't even on, and won't be until more work is done on the lines and it's passed inspection. My workmen are using a portable generator for their power tools."

"Noises? Lights?" Walter's eyes were enormous now.

"Don't be silly, Walter," Cookie scoffed. "There's no such thing as a ghost. You learned that in Hawaii."

"I wasn't sure a ghost would be good for my business," Nancy said, winking.

Cookie frowned thoughtfully. "Well, the story of Captain McKenna and his wife is certainly interesting. I wonder why they were such recluses, and if Mrs. McKenna really did suffocate in that fire."

"Maybe she died of a broken heart," Walter suggested. "From being lonely."

Cookie rolled her eyes at Nancy. "Walter is such a romantic."

Nancy laughed. "Well, it's a strange story, all right. And whatever damage the fire did was repaired. The house is in excellent shape as you can see."

They had reached the kitchen now where two workmen were cleaning paint brushes.

"I think we'll call it a day, Miss Merrit," one of them said. "We'll see you in the morning."

"Okay," Nancy replied. "I want to take my guests over to my little rental house, anyway." She ushered Mrs. McCorkle, Cookie, Walter, and Moriarty back to the big entryway.

"Can we see the upstairs?" Cookie asked.

"I think we should wait until tomorrow," Nancy replied. "You're probably hungry, so I thought we could go to one of the local fish restaurants for dinner rather than try to cook tonight."

"Sounds nice," Mrs. McCorkle said. "Both Cookie and Walter like fish."

"Some fish," Walter corrected her.

"Why don't you follow me in your car and we'll drop off your things," Nancy suggested. "Then we can wash up and go eat."

Nancy's rented house was only a couple of blocks away from the McKenna Mansion, and very small by comparison. There were only two bedrooms, and Cookie and Walter were given one with bunk beds.

"At least it has electricity," Nancy said with a laugh.

After everyone had cleaned up and Moriarty was left with a bowl of food in Nancy's kitchen, Cookie, Walter, and Mrs. McCorkle went with Nancy in her car to a restaurant down near the water.

"This place has excellent fish," Nancy said as they settled down with their menus. "I strongly recommend the fried squid."

"Squid!" Walter choked.

"Walter doesn't like tentacles," Cookie explained. "He's afraid they'll come alive and strangle him. But I'll try the squid."

"Then try the salmon, Walter," Nancy suggested.

"Yes, salmon, please," Walter echoed, looking relieved.

"I think I'll have salmon, too," Mrs. McCorkle added.

When the waitress had taken two orders of fried squid and two orders of baked salmon, Nancy and Mrs. McCorkle began to chat about their plans for the house while Cookie and Walter looked around the deserted restaurant.

"I think this town looks pretty dead," Cookie repeated to Walter in a low voice.

"Well, the McKennas are certainly dead," Walter said, grinning as if he had made a great joke.

"Walter, I'm afraid my father's sense of humor has taken ahold of you," Cookie said with a weary sigh. Then she stared off into space for a few minutes.

"I am rather curious about Captain Mc-

Kenna and his wife, though. Why would he build a house in this small town if he didn't want to make friends with anyone here?"

Just then the dinner orders arrived and everyone picked up their forks. Walter looked over at Cookie's plate.

"Those tentacles look just like someone fried a glob of rubber bands."

"Well, I can assure you they taste a lot better," Cookie said after she took a bite. "This is delicious."

"So is the salmon," Mrs. McCorkle added.

Everyone ate hungrily and afterward they went to an ice-cream parlor on the main street for dessert. Cookie and Walter ordered chocolate sundaes, and by the time they climbed back into Nancy's car Walter was practically asleep. Cookie, however, was alert and thinking about the McKenna mystery.

"Nancy, would you drive by the McKenna Mansion on the way home," Cookie asked. "I'd like to take a look at it at night."

"Sure," Nancy replied. "But you can't see much. There's no street light in front of the house."

Nancy and Mrs. McCorkle were so deep in conversation driving along the front of the house, they didn't look over. But Cookie squinted her eyes and looked out the window. Suddenly she gasped and grabbed Walter by the arm, jolting him awake.

"Wh . . . what . . . ?" Walter sputtered.

"Walter, I saw a light," she whispered.

"A light? What are you talking about?" Walter shook his head sleepily.

"I saw a light in one of the upstairs windows of the McKenna Mansion. It snapped on for just a second, then it went out."

"You're always telling me I'm imagining things," Walter grumbled. "Now you're imagining things."

"No, I am not!" Cookie hissed. "I'm positive I saw a light."

Back at Nancy's rented house, Cookie followed her mother and Nancy up the path to the front door while Walter trailed behind.

"Nancy," Cookie said, trying to make her voice sound casual, "what room is the upstairs right front of the McKenna Mansion?"

"Right front?" Nancy repeated. "Oh, that was Mrs. McKenna's room. It's quite pretty. I'll show it to you tomorrow."

The Investigation Starts

Cookie stopped short. Walter, who was staggering sleepily behind, tripped over her.

"What's the matter?" he mumbled.

"Walter, did you hear what Nancy just said?" Cookie spoke in a hushed tone. "The room where I saw the light was Mrs. McKenna's bedroom."

Walter blinked, trying to register the information.

"We've got to investigate that room tomorrow, Walter," Cookie said seriously.

When they were tucked in their bunks, Walter let out a long sigh. "Cookie," he said.

"Yes, Walter?"

"Are you sure there is no such thing as a ghost?"

"Of course, I'm sure. I believe that there are logical explanations for everything." She paused for a second. "Well, most everything. There *are* a few things that are impossible to explain logically. But this isn't one of them. Anyway, why would a ghost need to turn on a light?"

Walter thought for a minute. "Good point, Cookie. See you in the morning."

The next morning, Cookie and Walter were anxious to see the upstairs of the McKenna Mansion. Mrs. McCorkle, however, wanted to get started on Nancy's computer, so the two women decided to stay home and work.

"The back door will be open because the workmen are here," Nancy said to Cookie and Walter. "Go on in and look around. We'll be over when we want to take a break."

It was a bright, sunny morning and Cookie and Walter quickly walked the two blocks to the McKenna Mansion. Cookie had her magnifying glass in her pocket.

"I may need to examine Mrs. McKenna's bedroom very closely," she explained to Walter.

They circled around the house to the back door. Now that they could see the house in the daylight, they noticed another building on the back of the property.

"Is that a garage?" Walter asked.

"It must have been a carriage house," Cookie informed him. "They didn't have cars a hundred years ago, Walter. Remember? But fancy houses always had a building where buggies and wagons were kept."

Walter nodded. "Well, now it can be a garage."

The two workmen were painting in the kitchen when Cookie and Walter walked in the back door.

"Nancy said it would be all right if we looked around upstairs," Cookie explained.

"We've never been in a mansion before yesterday," Walter added.

"Make yourselves at home," one of the men said and resumed his work.

Cookie and Walter hurried into the entryway and then up the wide stairway that led to the second floor. There were a lot of doors leading off the upstairs landing, and for a minute Cookie was confused.

"Oh, that must be Mrs. McKenna's room," she said finally and raced down to the front of the house. She looked hesitantly at Walter before she turned the knob and walked in.

Nancy was right. It was a pretty room. The wallpaper, curtains, even the bedspread, were in excellent condition. Everything was in shades of soft green and peach, and the furniture was old-fashioned, lady-like and small in scale. Besides the bed there was a small bed table, a slim chest of drawers, and a little desk with a writing set that contained an inkwell, quill pen, and blotter.

"It looks as if Mrs. McKenna just stepped out for a minute," Cookie said.

"Yeah," Walter agreed, then he walked over to the fireplace and picked up an ornately framed photograph that was slightly faded with age.

"Do you think this was Mrs. McKenna?"

Cookie took the picture from Walter and studied it carefully.

"Probably," she replied. "She's quite young and very pretty. And she looks very serious."

"She looks sad," Walter commented. "Maybe she did die of a broken heart."

Cookie ignored Walter's last comment and took out her magnifying glass. She went over the objects in the room very carefully.

"Find anything?" Walter asked after a few minutes.

"Not yet," Cookie replied. Then she stopped suddenly. "Look at this, Walter," she said, pointing to the side window.

"Look at what?"

"See! The curtain has been caught in the window—as if it was closed in a hurry."

"So?"

"Well, it's very unlikely that Nancy would close the window so carelessly. These curtains are delicate. She would want to preserve them and therefore would be careful when she closed the window."

"Maybe she didn't notice?" Walter said.

Cookie shook her head. "She doesn't strike me as someone who wouldn't notice such things. My hunch is that someone was in this room in the last twenty-four hours and they opened and closed the window. Probably the same person who shined a light when we drove by last night."

"Are you sure you saw a light, Cookie?" Walter asked. "There aren't even any lamps in here, and we know the electricity isn't on yet."

"Walter, why are you arguing with me this morning?" Cookie said with annoyance. "It's not like you."

Walter grinned. "I'm just teasing you, Cookie."

Cookie shook her head slightly. Sometimes Walter had a very strange side to him.

"Something bothers me," Cookie said, as they were standing by the door. "There's something strange about this room, but I can't put my finger on it." She sighed and shook her head. "Well, let's take a look at the rest of the upstairs rooms now that we're here."

The two browsed around the upper floor for an hour, looking at all the bedrooms and the new bathrooms Nancy had added. They were both impressed by how nice the house was after a hundred years.

"I guess Nancy's uncle put in some of this newer-looking wallpaper," Cookie observed in one of the bedrooms. "But it sure goes well with the age and style of the house."

"Do you think many people will stop overnight at Bluff Bay?" Walter asked. "I only saw one motel when we drove into town."

Cookie shrugged. "I don't know how much business she'll get at first. But the highway outside of town is pretty busy and people have to stay somewhere. Maybe if she advertises that it's a bed-and-breakfast inn with a history people will be interested."

Walter raised his eyebrows slightly. "You mean a house with an unsolved mystery," he corrected her.

Nancy and Mrs. McCorkle had still not

arrived at the McKenna Mansion when Cookie and Walter went downstairs, so they decided to explore Bluff Bay a little.

"Let's go down to the waterfront," Cookie suggested. "I want to see if it's changed much since the days of Captain McKenna."

"Okay," Walter said agreeably.

The McKenna Mansion was only a couple of city blocks from a string of old warehouses across from the dock. Cookie studied the buildings.

"They don't look as if they've changed much in a hundred years," she said. "And they don't look like they're used for anything now."

"Yeah," Walter agreed. "It doesn't look as if there's much going on down there except for a few small fishing boats, and those bigger boats anchored out in the Bay."

"Let's walk along the dock," Cookie suggested, and Walter followed obediently as they strolled along the old wood plank dock of Bluff Bay. They were almost to the end when they saw a young man sanding the railing of a small fishing boat. He looked up when they stopped.

"Hi," he said. "Haven't seen you kids before. Just visiting Bluff Bay?"

Cookie nodded. "Yes, my mother's cousin

is opening up a bed-and-breakfast inn in the old McKenna Mansion, and my mom came to help her set up her bookkeeping system."

"And we came along for the ride," Walter added.

The young man cocked his head. "Find anything interesting in Bluff Bay?"

"Not too much," Cookie replied casually. She knew that a detective shouldn't discuss her observations with a stranger.

"But we don't believe the McKenna Mansion is haunted," Walter said hastily.

The young man laughed. "That's good. It might not be good for your cousin's business. By the way, my name's Mark."

"I'm Catherine McCorkle," Cookie said, "and this is Walter Sousa."

"Well, Catherine and Walter, I hope you find some excitement in Bluff Bay, but I wouldn't count on it."

"Thank you," Cookie said politely. "We'll try. Come on, Walter, we'd better get back to the McKenna Mansion. See you around, Mark."

"Yeah, bye," Walter said.

"He seemed friendly," Walter said, when they had walked back up the dock.

"Yes," Cookie replied. "But I bet he'd be

surprised if he knew we were investigating a hundred-year-old mystery."

"Is that what we're doing?" Walter asked.

"Well, doesn't it seem that there are a lot of unanswered questions about Captain and Mrs. McKenna," Cookie replied. "One: Why did Captain McKenna build a house in this town and bring a young wife here to become recluses? Two: What kind of a fire doesn't cause damage but suffocates a healthy woman? Three: Why did Captain McKenna pack up and leave a house he built and lived in for such a short time, and then never come back or try to sell it?"

"So I guess we *do* have another case, then, Cookie," Walter said.

"You might say that, Walter," Cookie replied quietly.

That evening back at Nancy's own house Cookie fixed them all hamburgers and, at Walter's request, some more coleslaw. Then Cookie and Walter watched television until it was time to go to bed.

Walter had already dropped off to sleep when Cookie decided she wanted a drink of water. She climbed out of her bunk carefully so that she wouldn't wake Walter and tiptoed into the kitchen. On the way back to bed, she passed by the room where Nancy and her mother were working on the computer.

"I have to admit I started out with some misgivings about the McKenna Mansion," Nancy was saying. Cookie decided to eavesdrop a bit.

"There was this talk about strange noises and lights in the house before I came to town. Then the first couple of weeks the workmen complained about their tools being misplaced when they came to work in the morning. And one morning I noticed the furniture had been rearranged in the parlor. The workmen were getting a little nervous, saying the house was haunted. But fortunately, this last week has gone very smoothly. I decided the workmen probably misplaced their own tools. Also, they moved the furniture around to work, and must have forgotten."

"You were probably just overly concerned about opening a new business," Mrs. McCorkle said in a soothing voice. "It's easy to imagine things."

"Probably," Nancy agreed.

Cookie sucked in her breath as she stared into the darkness of the hallway. Was Nancy really imagining things?

An Open Window

Cookie shivered slightly and hurried back to her bedroom. Walter was still sleeping soundly. She wanted to wake him and tell him about what she had overheard, but she decided to wait and talk to him in the morning. She knew Walter's imagination was huge and he might not be able to go back to sleep.

The next morning, Cookie did not have the opportunity to tell Walter about Nancy's comments until her mother and Nancy began working on the computer. When Cookie explained what she had heard the night before, Walter listened carefully.

"But she did say nothing had happened in the last week," Walter argued.

"Yes, but she doesn't know about the light I saw in Mrs. McKenna's window,"

Cookie said. "And she doesn't know about the curtain being caught in the window yesterday."

"I see what you mean, Cookie," Walter said slowly. "Strange things are still happening at the McKenna Mansion. She just hasn't noticed them."

Cookie nodded. "Exactly, and whoever is at the bottom of all this doesn't *want* her to notice them."

"I wonder what's going on?" Walter asked. "And why?"

"This has become more than a case of curiosity about the McKennas," Cookie said in a low, serious voice. "It's become a contemporary case, too."

"Contemporary?" Walter stumbled over the word.

"You know, something going on now," Cookie explained.

"Wow!" Walter exclaimed. "That means we've got two cases to solve now."

"Yes," Cookie said. "And we have to get moving. My plan is for us to sneak into the McKenna Mansion tonight and check out things by flashlight, maybe sit around a bit to see if anyone shows up."

Walter gulped. "You mean go in the house by ourselves?"

"Of course, Walter. We need more clues and information."

"But how are we going to get in the house? It's locked at night."

"I've already figured that out," Cookie replied. "Nancy always lays her keys on the kitchen table at night. We wait until my mother and Nancy are asleep, then we sneak in, get the keys, and go over to the McKenna Mansion. We'll be back before they wake up."

"Sounds pretty risky to me," Walter said.

"Walter, if I've told you more than once, I've told you a hundred times, a detective has to take risks."

"A hundred?" Walter questioned indignantly.

"Well—a dozen."

"Okay, okay," Walter said. "We'll sneak into the McKenna Mansion tonight."

"Meanwhile," Cookie continued, "let's take a walk down to the water again. The fresh air will clear our heads."

Cookie and Walter walked the short distance from the McKenna Mansion to the waterfront, studying the boats on the horizon as they strolled out onto the dock. Mark, the young man they had met the day before, was still working on his boat. He looked up and waved.

"Hi, Catherine, Walter. How's it going?"

"Pretty good," Walter replied.

Cookie shoved her straight red hair over her ears and squinted her eyes out at the Bay. "Do you know anything about that big boat out there, Mark? I noticed it before and it doesn't look like a fishing boat."

Mark looked off into the direction Cookie was pointing. "I don't know," he said. "Maybe it's a pleasure craft."

"Looks pretty big and serious for a pleasure craft," Cookie remarked.

"Cook . . . ah . . . Catherine is a detective," Walter explained quickly. "She has her own agency and she's already solved four big cases this summer."

"With Walter's help, of course," Cookie added. "He's my assistant."

Mark looked at them and nodded seriously. "That's very impressive. Find any good cases here in Bluff Bay?"

Cookie shook her head. "Things are pretty quiet here."

"Yeah, pretty quiet," Walter echoed.

Mark laughed. "I guess you'll have to think of this as a vacation and wait until you get back to the city to find another case."

"Guess so," Cookie agreed. "Well, see you around, Mark."

Mark waved to them and Cookie and Walter walked back up the dock.

"Wouldn't he be surprised if he knew what we were doing?" Walter said with a chuckle.

"He certainly would," Cookie agreed.

That evening, Mrs. McCorkle suggested they all go out to dinner at the fish restaurant again.

"Isn't that kind of expensive, Mom?" Cookie said. "I could fix something here for half the price."

"Oh, this is a vacation," Mrs. McCorkle replied. "Besides, the restaurants here are not nearly as expensive as they are in the city."

"Okay," Cookie said. "I'm all for it." And she and Walter ordered fried shrimp this time.

When they returned to Nancy's house, Cookie and Walter pretended to be very tired and went to their bedroom to get ready for bed.

"Just take off your shoes, Walter," Cookie ordered. "And get in bed with your clothes on. Pull the covers up under your chin so my mother can't tell we're dressed when she comes in to say good night."

A few minutes later Mrs. McCorkle found Cookie and Walter nearly asleep, blankets tucked up under their chins.

"This fresh sea air must be good for you two," she whispered and kissed them both good night.

"Okay, Walter," Cookie whispered, after her mother had closed the door behind her. "Pinch yourself to stay awake. Mom and Nancy will go to bed soon. I know they're tired from working on that computer."

Cookie counted the minutes until the house grew quiet, then crept out of her bunk and shook Walter's shoulder. He had almost fallen asleep.

"Put on your shoes and stay here with Moriarty, Walter. I'm going to see if Mom and Nancy are asleep, then I'll get the keys to the McKenna Mansion."

Cookie opened the door quietly and tiptoed down the hall. She paused in front of the other bedroom and waited a few seconds. Satisfied with the silence, she slipped into the kitchen and shined her flashlight on the table. The keys were there. Within minutes, she was back in the bedroom where Walter was sitting groggily on the edge of his bunk, trying to tie his shoelaces.

"All clear, Walter. You carry Moriarty. We can't leave him here because he's awake and might start barking for us."

Moriarty jumped up into Walter's arms as if he understood completely, and Walter staggered out the door after Cookie.

"Shhh." She put her finger to her lips as they passed the other bedroom and out the back door. In a few seconds they were out on the street.

"It sure is windy tonight," Walter said, holding Moriarty close to him.

"I heard Nancy say she thought the weather was going to be stormy," Cookie responded. "Probably a little rain but a lot of thunder and lightning though."

As they rounded the corner to the Mc-Kenna Mansion, Cookie and Walter looked up at Mrs. McKenna's bedroom window. A light flashed off.

"Quick," Cookie urged, making a dash for the front door. But it took her several seconds to find the right key and she fumbled to unlock it.

"Upstairs!" Cookie commanded, racing up the long stairway while Walter, with Moriarty in his arms, stumbled after her.

Cookie burst into Mrs. McKenna's room, but the light was definitely off. Walter stood panting in the doorway, partly from exhaustion, partly from fear. Cookie flashed her light around the room, but could see nothing. She even looked under the bed, but there was no one in the room.

"Look!" Walter exclaimed in a breathy voice. "The window! It's wide open!"

Cookie swung around toward the side window. Sure enough it was open and the curtain was blowing in the wind. She ran to the window and looked out.

"No one would dare jump out of here," she said. "They'd break their neck." She turned and looked back at Walter, her flashlight making an eerie pattern on the bedroom wall.

"Someone was here just a few minutes ago. They left the light on and the window open, but where did they go?"

"Maybe . . ." Walter coughed nervously. "Maybe they are still in the house."

Trouble in the Night

Cookie was silent for a second, then she charged past Walter and out the bedroom door.

"Come on, Walter," she said. "We have to search the house quickly. Although they probably got away by now."

Moriarty, who had picked up on Walter's fear, wrapped his paws around his neck so that Walter could only talk in a muffled voice.

"Cookie, what if they have a gun?"

Cookie stopped in the hallway and turned to Walter. Her expression was determined. She took a deep breath.

"How do they know *we* don't have a gun?"

"Kids don't carry guns, Cookie." Walter's voice rose on a note of hysteria.

Cookie didn't answer. Instead, she

opened the door of the next bedroom and flashed her light around. Then she walked over to the closet and flung it open, half expecting to find someone crouching inside. But the closet was empty. She proceeded to go through each bedroom and bathroom upstairs while Walter and Moriarty quivered in the doorways. But the upstairs was empty of people.

"Let's search the downstairs," Cookie said finally, and started back downstairs.

"Look, we left the front door wide open," Walter said. "Whoever was here could have run out of Mrs. McKenna's room, hid somewhere, then run out the front door while we were upstairs."

"But how did that person get in?" Cookie asked. "I'm sure the back door is locked. Let's check."

Cookie, Walter, and Moriarty searched the entire first floor, but found no one, nor any evidence that anyone had run through the house. And the back door was locked. Finally, standing by the front door, Cookie turned to Walter and stared at him. He was still holding Moriarty. He looked back at her intently, his eyes wide.

"Don't say it, Walter!"

"I won't, Cookie. I won't say anything

about the McKenna Mansion being haunted." Then he grinned.

Cookie smiled. She had to admit that even when Walter was scared he managed to keep a sense of humor.

"Come on," she said. "We'd better get back home and into bed. We've got a lot of work to do tomorrow."

Walter didn't ask what kind of work. He didn't want to know.

Both Cookie and Walter were glad to be back home under the covers. The wind was strong and cold and the walk home dark and spooky. They both fell asleep, exhausted. Apparently, Mrs. McCorkle had not heard them leave or come in, for when she walked into their bedroom the next day, she called them sleepyheads.

"You children are certainly getting a good rest," Mrs. McCorkle remarked. "This vacation has been good for you. You've solved enough cases this summer."

Cookie and Walter exchanged brief glances, but said nothing. Later that morning, Cookie said to Walter, "I think we should spend the afternoon at the McKenna Mansion and go over it more carefully."

"Aren't those workmen going to think

we're weird?" Walter asked. "How many normal kids hang around a Victorian mansion day after day?"

Cookie frowned, then snapped her fingers. "I've got it. I'll make some chili and take it over to them for lunch. That will put them in a good mood and they'll think we're there to watch them."

"Well, okay," Walter agreed reluctantly.

"Excuse me," Cookie said as she went into the bedroom where her mother and Nancy were hunched over the computer. "I'm sorry to interrupt, but I decided to make some chili for lunch. I haven't done much cooking since I arrived, so I thought it would be nice to take a hot lunch over to Nancy's workmen."

"What a nice idea!" Nancy exclaimed. "They'll love it. They seem to have huge appetites."

"Shall I make enough for you two?" Cookie asked.

Mrs. McCorkle smiled. "I think I'll just have a salad and some fruit, dear. I've been eating a lot lately."

"Me, too," Nancy echoed.

"Then I'll just make enough for four," Cookie said. "Do you mind if I use that ground beef in the refrigerator, Nancy?"

"Help yourself to anything, Cookie."

Cookie paused a minute outside the bedroom. She was trying to decide what she was going to put in the chili. She heard Nancy talking to her mother.

"Such nice children. They seem to be able to amuse themselves so well."

Mrs. McCorkle laughed. "You can say that again. At least they're not off solving another detective case. This quiet little town has been good for them."

Cookie smiled to herself and returned to the kitchen where Walter was reading the funnies in the morning paper.

"Okay, Walter, let's get to work on the chili."

For the next half hour, Cookie and Walter worked to put together a pot of chili. Walter chopped while Cookie sautéed. Then Cookie browned the meat while Walter opened a can of beans and a can of tomatoes. Finally, the chili was simmering on the stove and Cookie took off her apron. Walter had just finished washing pots and pans.

"Let's put four bowls and four spoons in a sack, Walter," Cookie said. "Then I'll wrap the chili pot in a towel so we can carry it over to the McKenna Mansion. We probably should take along some crackers, too."

Within minutes, Cookie, Walter, and Moriarty were on their way down the street. Cookie carried the chili while Walter brought the bowls and spoons. When they walked in the back door, the workmen were painting the trim in the dining room.

"Hey, something smells good," the tall man called out.

"We made some chili for your lunch," Cookie said. "We thought maybe you'd like a hot lunch for a change . . ."

"Hey, that's great, kid," the other man said. "I really do like chili."

Cookie and Walter set up the table in the kitchen and sat down to eat with the men, who showed their appreciation by eating hungrily.

"This is great!"

"Did you make this yourself? You're just a kid."

"I do almost all the cooking in my house," Cookie said.

"And I eat almost every meal there," Walter added.

"I don't blame you!" the tall man said. "You kids can cook for me anytime."

After lunch, Cookie and Walter rinsed the dishes while the men went back to work.

"Mind if we hang around a while?" Cookie asked. "We don't have much to do at home."

"Go right ahead."

Cookie and Walter went upstairs with Moriarty trailing behind. They went first to Mrs. McKenna's room. The door was open as they had left it and so was the window.

"I should have closed it last night," Cookie said, shutting the window firmly. "All this wind is blowing dust on those beautiful curtains."

They were just closing the door to Mrs. McKenna's room when she paused to take a last careful look around.

"I wish I knew what it is that bothers me about this room," Cookie said. Then she shook her head and started down the hall.

All afternoon, Cookie and Walter tramped around the McKenna Mansion. They even went up into the dark and stuffy attic, which was full of old boxes. It wasn't until Cookie glanced at her watch that she realized how the hours had slipped by.

"I guess we'd better go back downstairs," she said. "The workmen will want to go home."

In the kitchen, the men were cleaning up after painting. Cookie and Walter walked outside with them and chatted while the men washed their brushes. Finally, Cookie went back inside and picked up the chili pot. Walter took the dishes.

Cookie and Walter, with Moriarty following, walked back home slowly. They were both disappointed at not being able to find any clues to what was going on at the McKenna Mansion.

"We'll just have to keep looking," Cookie said.

Walter nodded. "Yeah, we can't get discouraged."

That night, Cookie and Walter went to bed early. This time they both fell asleep quickly, tired from the night before and from the day of investigating. Sometime in the night they were both awakened by pounding on the front door. They bolted out of bed and were met in the hall by Nancy and Mrs. McCorkle. Nancy opened the door to find both a fireman and a policeman looking at her grimly.

"Miss Merrit," the fireman said, "there has been a fire at the McKenna Mansion."

"Oh, no!" Nancy gasped.

"Don't worry, ma'am," he added quickly. "There was only some minor damage to the old carriage house. Someone saw the flames and called us in time. We were able to put it out with little damage to that building and none to the house."

"Oh, thank heavens!" Nancy exclaimed.

"But Miss Merrit," the policeman said sternly, "we think you should talk to your workmen. We feel the fire was started by lightning striking a trash can full of paint rags. If they aren't more careful, there could be some real damage. With this strange weather we're having, we're gonna get more thunder and lightning."

"I certainly will talk to them," Nancy said hotly. "I can't believe they weren't more careful."

After the policeman and fireman had left and Cookie and Walter were ushered off to bed, Cookie looked over the edge of her bunk at Walter.

"It wasn't their fault," she whispered.

"Whose fault?"

"The workmen," Cookie replied. "Remember, we watched them clean their rags, then rinse them in water. They wouldn't catch on fire if they were wet. Besides that trash barrel wasn't anywhere near the carriage house."

"Hey, you're right," Walter said.

"Someone else started that fire," Cookie said in a low voice.

An Important Connection

Walter was silent for a few seconds, then he whispered to Cookie, "Do you think the person who turned on the light and left the window open in Mrs. McKenna's room is the same person who started the fire tonight?"

"Well, think about it, Walter," Cookie replied, trying to keep her voice low. "Strange things are going on at the McKenna Mansion, and they must be connected. It's only logical."

"Wow!"

"But don't think about it anymore tonight, Walter. We need to get some sleep."

"Okay," Walter responded.

Cookie lay awake until she heard Walter breathing evenly. She was forming a plan in her mind, but she didn't want to discuss it with Walter until morning. It would make him much too nervous.

"I don't think I'm going to say anything to the workmen," Nancy announced at the breakfast table. "Since this is a weekend they won't be back until Monday and they've finished painting now, anyway. I made a decision to get the house opened for business soon and I don't want to take the chance of making them angry by accusing them of carelessness."

"I think that's a good idea." Cookie spoke in her most thoughtful, adult voice. "Walter and I have been around the house long enough to see that those men work hard and fast. They're not usually careless."

"Not at all," Walter added firmly.

"There's a little theater in the next town that is opening a play in two weeks," Nancy continued. "It brings in people from all over the area on the weekends, and I'd really like to be ready for business then."

"Well, the house is almost finished," Mrs. McCorkle said. "And in a couple more days we'll have this bookkeeping system set up."

Nancy smiled. "I really appreciate all your help."

"You know, Nancy," Cookie said, as if the

idea were just occurring to her, "why don't Walter and I sleep in the McKenna Mansion until we leave? We don't care if there isn't any electricity. It would be like camping out and we'd be sort of caretakers, wouldn't we, Walter?"

Looking straight at Walter, Cookie kicked him under the table. His mouth, which had dropped open in astonishment, suddenly snapped shut in pain.

"Won't we, Walter?" she repeated.

"Ah . . . ah . . . yeah," Walter stammered.

Nancy looked at Mrs. McCorkle. "Well, that's a nice idea. I'm not sure we need caretakers now that the paint rags aren't around, but it might be fun for you kids. I could put a couple of mattresses down on the library floor, along with two sleeping bags I have. There's a phone installed in there. You could always call us if you got lonely."

"Oh, we won't get lonely," Cookie assured her quickly. "What do you say, Mom? We can take over a thermos of hot chocolate and have some popcorn. We could play cards by flashlight. It'll be cozy and fun."

She glanced over at Walter, who looked as if someone was just about to be hanged.

"Why not?" Mrs. McCorkle replied. "It does sound like fun."

After Nancy and Mrs. McCorkle had gone back to the computer, Cookie grinned at Walter.

"Great idea, huh?"

"If you like going to your own funeral, yeah," Walter muttered.

"Oh, come on, Walter. Nothing's going to happen to us. No one will even know we're there, but we can keep an eye on the house, especially Mrs. McKenna's room. If we hear noises we'll. . . ."

"Call the police," Walter interrupted.

"Okay, we'll call the police," Cookie consented. "But someone has to catch the person or persons *at* the house. We just don't have enough clues to figure out who's doing all these things and why. Don't you agree?"

"I don't want to talk about it anymore," Walter said. "I feel as if I have only a few hours to live and I want to enjoy them."

Cookie smiled and rolled her eyes. "Oh, Walter, you're so dramatic."

That evening, armed with a thermos of hot chocolate, a bowl of popcorn, and a deck of cards, Cookie, Walter, and Moriarty sat on Nancy's sleeping bags in the McKenna Mansion library. They had helped Nancy lug in the mattresses and now she was leaving to go work on the computer.

"I've locked the back door and the phone is right there on the desk if you get scared or lonely," Nancy reminded them. "I'll lock the front door as I leave."

"We'll be fine," Cookie assured her. "We'll see you in the morning."

"I hope you can sleep in all this wind and thunder," Nancy said.

"Oh, we always sleep hard," Cookie said. "Don't we, Walter?"

"Always," Walter echoed in a weak voice.

After Nancy had gone, Cookie poured them each a cup of hot chocolate.

"Are we going to stay up all night, Cookie?" Walter asked.

"Well, I'm going to try. I've left the library door slightly open so I can hear anything that goes on if I doze. And you know Moriarty. He has great ears."

"I won't be able to go to sleep tonight," Walter said. "I'm too terrified."

"Oh, Walter," Cookie soothed, "let's just play Fish and talk about other things."

They drank hot chocolate and ate popcorn while they played a couple of games of Fish. Then they crawled into their sleeping bags, fully dressed, but with their shoes off. Cookie turned off the flashlight.

"Would you like me to tell you *The Ad-*

venture of the Speckled Band?" Cookie asked. "It's my favorite Sherlock Holmes case."

"Is it scary?" Walter asked.

"You be the judge," Cookie replied, and began retelling one of her favorite detective's famous legends. She spoke softly and steadily, and it wasn't long before she could tell that Walter was asleep. Soon, she could feel her eyelids getting very heavy.

Suddenly, Cookie sat upright. She realized a noise had awakened her. She listened again, but it was hard to hear over the wind.

Careful not to wake Moriarty, who was on the foot of her sleeping bag, Cookie stood up. She looked over at Walter. He was sleeping soundly and snoring slightly. She thought for a minute, then decided against waking him. With her flashlight in hand, Cookie tiptoed to the library door and opened it wide. She could hear the noises better now, and she was certain they were coming from Mrs. McKenna's room.

Cookie crept slowly up the stairs in her stocking feet. She didn't dare use her flashlight, but an occasional flash of lightning lit up the house. She could feel her heart pounding in her chest and she wondered if she should have done what she had promised Walter—call the police.

By the time Cookie reached the second floor landing, the noises had stopped. She continued along the hallway until she came to the door of Mrs. McKenna's bedroom. It was shut. She turned the knob very slowly and the door opened easily.

Cookie sucked in her breath. There were no sounds coming from the room now, so she opened the door wider, reluctant to risk turning on her flashlight. Suddenly, a burst of lightning lit up the room. She could see it was empty, although the side window was open again. Cookie raced to the window and looked out. She could make out the faint outline of a truck in front of the house. The engine started up and she turned for the door. She wanted to get downstairs in time to see the truck more clearly, but in her haste she tripped over the little table next to Mrs. McKenna's bed and sent herself and the table sprawling.

Furious with her own clumsiness, Cookie heard the sound of the truck driving away. She turned on her light to set the table back up when she noticed one of the drawers had fallen out and flipped upside down. A small

book was lying on the floor beside it. In putting the drawer back she realized it had a false bottom. The book must have fallen from a secret compartment. Cookie picked up the little worn volume and turned her flashlight on the first page. It read:

Property of Ardeth McKenna,
September 1890

Cookie's mouth dropped open. She had found Mrs. McKenna's personal diary. She set the little table upright next to the bed and hurried downstairs and into the library. Walter was still asleep and Moriarty had not moved.

"So much for your ears, Moriarty," Cookie muttered.

She crawled back into her sleeping bag and opened the diary. She studied Mrs. McKenna's faint, formal script with her flashlight. Cookie read steadily for an hour until she suddenly gasped. She reached over and grabbed Walter by the shoulder to wake him.

"Wha . . . what is it?" Walter sat up in his sleeping bag. "What happened? Did you hear a noise? Call the police!"

"Walter, hush! Just listen to me!" Cookie exclaimed. "This house has a secret passageway."

The Mystery Unravels

Walter looked puzzled, so Cookie continued. "See, Walter. I heard this noise a little while ago. I was sure it was coming from Mrs. McKenna's room. You and Moriarty were asleep, so I went upstairs to check. I . . ."

"You went up alone!" Walter interrupted.

"There wasn't enough time to call the police, Walter. I need to catch the person in the act."

"The act of what?" Walter demanded.

"I don't know," Cookie said, impatiently. "Just let me explain."

Cookie related to Walter what had happened up until she got back to the library with the diary. Walter was fascinated. Even Moriarty seemed to be listening.

"I've read Mrs. McKenna's dairy through. It's sort of boring because she led such a boring life. Her husband never let her have any friends and they never had any company. She had to spend all her time with Captain McKenna's mean old sister. Finally, she asked her husband if she could move into the front bedroom because it was more cheerful, but secretly she wanted to be able to look out the window and see people walking by. He finally gave in, but when she moved into the bedroom she began to feel even worse. She was tired and fuzzy in the mornings and she complained of strange dreams."

Cookie paused and took a deep breath. "Well, one night, after she decided not to drink the evening tea her husband's sister always brought her, she found herself sleeping very lightly. She realized she had been drugged before, so this night when she heard a noise she opened her eyes wide. Seeing the fireplace move, she watched as her husband came out, followed by some strange men."

"What? The fireplace opened?" Walter looked at Cookie in astonishment.

"Yes, Walter. A secret passageway is behind the fireplace," Cookie replied excitedly. "That's what was bothering me about that room. There is a fireplace, hearth, and all. But there's no chimney on that side of the

64

house. It's obviously a fake fireplace to cover up the entrance to a secret passageway. Mrs. McKenna said her husband was using it to smuggle in gold."

"Where do you suppose it goes?" Walter asked.

Cookie shook her head. "I don't know, Walter, but we have to find out how to open the fireplace and follow the passageway. I'm sure the mystery will be solved then. . . ." Cookie stopped and frowned.

"Well, that part of the mystery will be solved. I still don't know if Mrs. McKenna suffocated in that fire. According to her diary, she was so upset by this discovery she decided she was going to escape from here forever. She was going to make a rope out of her blankets and sheets and let herself down from the window and run away. She didn't really have any place to go, though. Her father had once been very rich, then lost all his money. Captain McKenna had paid Mrs. McKenna's father's debts on the condition he could marry his daughter. Mrs. McKenna knew her husband would come looking for her if she went home."

"Well, what do you suppose happened then?" Walter demanded, totally involved in the story now.

"Who knows, Walter? That's where the diary ends. I guess we'll just have to accept the story about her suffocating in a fire." Cookie sighed. "At least we have a chance to find out what's going on at the McKenna Mansion now. It's obvious that the person who has been turning on the light in Mrs. McKenna's bedroom and leaving the window open knows about the secret passageway. That's how they get in and out. And that truck has to have something to do with all this, too."

"Let me see the diary, Cookie."

Cookie handed Walter the flashlight, then tossed the diary lightly onto his sleeping bag. In the process, something metal dropped out and onto the floor. Walter reached over and picked it up.

"What was that?" Cookie asked.

"It's a key," Walter replied. He turned the item over in his hand. "A crooked key, and it looks very old. It fell out of the diary."

Walter looked at the diary carefully. He flipped open the pages and then held it up for Cookie to see.

"Look! The back cover has a little slot where the key fits in. You must not have noticed it. It was probably tucked way down

and then worked itself loose when you tossed it to me."

Together, Cookie and Walter examined the back of the book and the key.

"It must be the key to the passageway," Cookie exclaimed. "It's very strange looking—not like any key I've ever seen."

"We'll have to wait until morning to find out how it works," Walter said. "It's too dark in that room now."

"I don't think we should waste any time, Walter," Cookie said. "No telling what this person will do next. We should go upstairs now and use the flashlight to look at that fireplace. Put on your shoes."

Walter swallowed hard. "Okay, but I'd rather wait until daylight."

Cookie ignored Walter's plea as she tied the laces on her sneakers. Walter picked up Moriarty and the three of them hurried upstairs. Mrs. McKenna's bedroom was just as Cookie had left it. She walked over and closed the window. The wind was still howling and the room had grown cold.

"I'm sure it was because of the wind that I couldn't hear what was going on in that room until it was too late," Cookie said.

"Maybe the wind saved you from danger," Walter said.

"Maybe," Cookie said, "but I'd sure like to know what that truck was doing here."

Cookie shined her light over the fireplace and Walter ran his hands down the edge of the structure.

"I wish Mrs. McKenna had said something about the key," Cookie said.

"Maybe she was too smart," Walter said.

"Or maybe she hid the key in her diary and put it in the secret compartment so that no one would ever find it," Cookie argued.

"How do you suppose the person who's been here is getting into the passageway then?" Walter asked.

"I think they must have come on it from the other end. The fireplace probably opens from the other side, too," Cookie said. "All they would have to do is not let it swing shut while they were in here."

Walter nodded as he continued to feel around the fireplace. "Good logic, Cookie."

"Just a hunch, Walter." Cookie tried to make her tone sound modest, but she was secretly pleased with her reasoning.

"Stand back a minute, Cookie," Walter said suddenly. "O.K. Shine the light slowly around the edge of the fireplace. I want to check something."

Cookie did as Walter asked. She circled the entire fireplace carefully with her light, pausing now and then for Walter to study it. Finally, Walter grabbed her hand.

"There! Focus the light on that part that looks like a bear claw." Then he said, "Do the same thing on the other side."

Cookie concentrated on the claw on the other side of the fireplace now. Walter stared at it for a minute, then snapped his fingers.

"That's it! This claw is different from the one in the middle and the one on the other side. Bring the flashlight over closer."

Cookie moved over to the fireplace and shined her light on the ornate claw that, along with the other two, appeared to be holding up the mantel of the fireplace. Walter ran his hand slowly over the finished wood until he finally found what he was looking for.

"Look, Cookie," he cried excitedly, "this little piece of wood behind the claw swings away."

Cookie moved the light closer. Walter had moved a little piece of wood to one side, revealing a small opening. Now he slipped in the key. Its crooked shape fit perfectly in the space. He turned the key and stepped back. The fireplace swung open to reveal a large opening. Cookie and Walter shivered as they looked down into the darkness. They had found the secret passageway in the Mc-Kenna Mansion!

Discovery and Surprise

"We found it, Walter!" Cookie felt like shouting, but she kept her voice down. She was afraid someone might be lurking down below.

Walter nodded. His eyes were blinking rapidly in the ray of Cookie's flashlight. "Now what?"

"Stay right here with Moriarty," Cookie said. "I'll be right back."

Cookie dashed out of the room and pounded down the stairs, leaving a very scared Walter standing next to the dark hole in the wall of Mrs. McKenna's bedroom. She was back in a few minutes with Moriarty's leash.

"Look, Cookie," Walter said. "You were right. There's a latch on the other side of the fireplace. A person can get in easily from the opposite side."

"Uh huh," Cookie responded absently. She was busy untangling Moriarty's leash. "Now, Walter, you put this on Moriarty while I shine the light for you. We can't take him down into the passageway because he might bark and call attention to us. I'll fasten the leash to the bedpost."

Walter had already started to hook the leash onto Moriarty's collar. Now he stopped and stared at Cookie.

"Go down into that hole? Are you kidding?"

"We have to, Walter. It's the only way we'll find out where it leads and solve this case."

"But . . . but, Cookie. . . ." Walter's hands trembled as he clipped the leash onto the little dog's collar. "That could be very dangerous, Cookie."

Cookie just looked at him. Finally, Walter sighed and nodded.

"I know, a detective has to expect danger."

"I'll go first, Walter," Cookie said. "I can see a ladder that's attached to the wall of the passageway. You shine the light down on me."

Cookie slipped Moriarty's leash over Mrs. McKenna's bedpost and knelt down. She looked sternly at the little terrier.

"Now, you can't bark, Moriarty. You could

73

get Walter and me into big trouble. We won't be gone long."

She stood up. "I think he understands. Now, Walter, I'm going down, so light my way."

Walter flashed the light on Cookie as she crouched down and stepped on the first rung of the ladder. Cautiously, she lowered herself down, rung by rung, until she reached bottom.

"I'm on solid ground now, Walter," she called out in a hushed voice. "It's about twenty feet straight down. Toss the light down to me and I'll hold it on you. It's pitch black down here."

Walter dropped the flashlight down and Cookie managed to catch it. Then she shined it up at him. She could see his wide, scared eyes.

"Come on, Walter. The ladder is very solid."

Walter started down. He moved very slowly and by the time he reached bottom, Cookie was tapping her foot impatiently.

"Here, Walter. Hold the flashlight on me. I want to see how big this passageway is."

Cookie stretched out her arms while Walter illuminated her movement. She turned to him and nodded.

"Just as I figured. It's not wide, about four feet wide and about six feet high. Now we have to find out how far it goes."

Walter didn't say anything. Cookie could tell that he was too scared to talk, so she took the light from him and started down the passageway. She had only gone a short way when her light flashed on a door on the left. She stopped and ran the light over it. Then she took ahold of the metal bolt that was securing it.

"Come on, Walter, help me open this door."

"What if the bad guys are in there?" Walter's voice quavered.

Cookie cast a stern look at Walter who then moved forward and helped her tug at the bolt. Soon the two of them were able to lift it up and open the door. They stepped back as it swung open. Cookie flashed her light around inside. It was a large room, lined with boxes that were covered with plastic. Cookie stepped inside the doorway and Walter followed behind her.

"Whew!" she said. "What's that odor?"

"It smells like a barnyard," Walter said. "Or a chicken coop."

Cookie walked over to one of the boxes and lifted up the plastic. There was a wild squawk and she dropped the cover.

75

"It's a cage!" she exclaimed.

"That was a macaw, I think," Walter said. "I saw this television documentary on parrots and there was a macaw that was the same color."

Cookie lifted the plastic up slightly and studied a small label on the bottom of the cage.

"You're right, Walter. It says here that it's a 'Hyacinth Macaw,' and it's from Brazil. It says its plummage is cobalt blue."

Cookie and Walter moved over to another cage and lifted the plastic enough to read another label.

"This is a 'Golden Conere' from northeastern Brazil," Walter said.

"And this is a 'Glossy Cockatoo' from Australia." Cookie was looking at another cage.

The children were careful not to lift the plastic too high and disturb the birds as they walked around the room for several minutes, reading the labels on the cages. They found the names of a dozen or more rare birds from Australia and Latin America. Finally Cookie turned and looked at Walter.

"You know what this is? Exotic-bird smuggling. I heard about this on the news. There's big money in it."

"Someone discovered Captain McKenna's

76

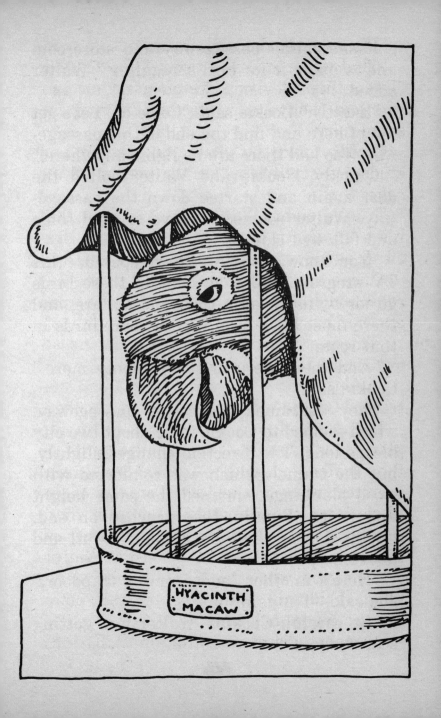

HYACINTH
MACAW

gold-smuggling passageway and storeroom and is using it for bird smuggling," Walter added.

"Exactly," Cookie said. "Come on. Let's get out of here and find the end of this passageway. Too bad there are no lights anywhere."

Quickly, Cookie and Walter bolted the door again and started down the passageway. Walter seemed to have relaxed some and followed closely.

"You know, Cookie," he whispered, "this TV program said that some of these birds go for as much as a thousand dollars, and there must have been fifty or more birds in that room."

"And there were probably plenty more," Cookie said.

They continued along the passageway, which seemed to Cookie to be about two city blocks long. The direction changed slightly, but the tunnel, which was reinforced with wood planking, remained the same height and width. Finally, they reached an end. Cookie flashed the light along the wall and above her.

"Here's another ladder and a trapdoor," she said. "I'm going up."

"Be careful, Cookie." Walter was getting scared again.

Cookie handed him the flashlight so he could illuminate her climb. When she reached the top, Cookie pushed gently on the trapdoor, and to her surprise it opened easily. She whispered down to Walter, "Hand me the light."

Walter climbed up a few rungs and passed the flashlight to Cookie who shined it through the crack. She snapped it off, climbed back down in the dark and stood panting for a minute. Then she spoke.

"It's one of those old warehouses down by the dock," she said. "It's a perfect place for a smuggling operation because the goods can come in by boat and get transferred directly into the warehouse and down the passageway. Someone must be smuggling in those birds and lowering them out the window of Mrs. McKenna's room at night. That's what that truck was doing—waiting to get the birds."

At that moment, the trapdoor above them was flung back. Cookie and Walter instinctively shrank back in the shadowy corner and held their breath. Cookie could see two men above them, but Walter was covering his eyes.

"Wait," one man said, "we'd better leave things just as they are tonight. Those kids are still in the house and if they hear any more noise, they might call the police."

"Then we've got to move everything out tomorrow night," the other man said. "It's getting too risky."

Cookie could hear him curse under his breath.

"If only those snoopy little brats hadn't shown up. I figured we had a couple more weeks to transport before the Inn opened. We could have gotten everything off the boat by then."

They dropped the door and it slammed shut. Cookie and Walter waited a minute or two, then Cookie grabbed Walter's arm and dragged him back down the passageway. She didn't turn the light on until they had groped along for several yards. Then she snapped it on and they ran the rest of the way. Cookie pushed Walter up the ladder, shining the light for him, then she followed. When they were safely inside Mrs. McKenna's bedroom, Cookie and Walter both pushed the fireplace back in place. Cookie took the key out of the lock and put it in her pocket. Moriarty, who had been waiting patiently, did not bark when he saw them but wagged his tail instead. Walter unhooked his leash and the three of them left the room quickly and closed the door. It wasn't until they were back in the library that either of the children spoke.

"Whew! That was close," Cookie said as she threw herself back on her sleeping bag. "Really close."

"I thought we were done for," Walter said, and he let out a huge sigh of relief.

Cookie sat up again and looked over at him. "Walter, did you recognize the voice of one of those men?"

"No."

Cookie was silent for a minute, then she said in a low voice, "It was Mark, Walter, that fisherman we met down by the dock."

Cookie and Walter
Ask for Help

Walter's jaw dropped open. "So he's not really a fisherman then?"

"Well, he may do a little fishing but only to look as if he's working. He's really here as an accomplice to the other guy on that big boat out in the Bay. Remember I said it didn't look like a pleasure boat? It's probably full of birds."

"Wow!" was all Walter could say.

Cookie glanced at her watch. "We'd better try to get some sleep, Walter. We're going to have to stop those two from smuggling out the rest of the birds tomorrow night. They have to be caught in the act."

Walter turned to Cookie and stared grimly at her. "Cookie, I'm putting my foot down. . . ."

"Don't bother, Walter, don't bother." Cookie waved away his protest. "I'm not planning to do it myself. We'll go to the local police in the morning and tell them. These men have to be arrested on the spot."

"Whew!" Walter said and crawled into his sleeping bag. "For a minute, I thought you were going to try to stop them single-handed . . . I mean double-handed."

Cookie sighed. "I sure wish I could be there, Walter. I'd like to be under Mrs. McKenna's bed when they're arrested."

Walter, who was exhausted from running and being scared, fell asleep immediately. Cookie drifted off quickly, too, and didn't wake up until her mother and Nancy came into the library in the morning.

"My gosh, you two are sure lazy this morning," Mrs. McCorkle said as she leaned over to give Cookie a kiss. "I haven't seen you children so relaxed all summer."

Cookie sat up with a start. "What time is it?"

"Almost nine o'clock," Mrs. McCorkle replied. "Put on your shoes and brush your teeth. Nancy bought some hot cinnamon rolls at the bakery and I've fixed some fruit. We'll have a nice Sunday morning breakfast at the McKenna Bed-and-Breakfast Inn."

Mrs. McCorkle then disappeared out the library door.

"Rats," Cookie grumbled. "I wanted to get down to the police station early. Now we'll have to wait until Nancy and Mom go back to the house."

"We still have all day, Cookie. Those guys said they wouldn't try to transport the birds until night."

"Yeah, but the cops might want to call in the FBI," Cookie said in a loud whisper. "Smuggling isn't just a local crime."

"They might call the FBI? Wow!" Walter exclaimed.

Cookie and Walter were surprised at how hungry they were after a night of work. They ate quickly while Nancy told them about the call she'd had from a hotel in the next town.

"They want to refer my Inn for the theater weekends," she said. "I'm so glad I'll be ready. Thanks to your mother, Cookie, the Inn will open with no problems. It's been so easy."

Cookie glanced at Walter but said nothing. She encouraged Nancy and her mother to leave when they were finished with breakfast.

"Go on back to work," she said. "You probably have some last-minute things to do on the computer and Walter and I can clean up the kitchen. We love it here. We slept like rocks."

"I'll say you did," Cookie's mother laughed. "Wait until your father hears that you managed to get through a week without solving another detective case. He won't believe it."

After Nancy and Mrs. McCorkle left, Cookie and Walter quickly tidied up the kitchen. Then they headed down the street toward the main section of town.

"I looked up the address of the police station," Cookie said. "It's on Bay Street near the fish restaurant where we had dinner."

It didn't take long to locate the little brick police station and Cookie, Walter, and Moriarty hurried up the steps. In the reception area they saw two young policeman sitting at desks going through some papers.

"Excuse me," Cookie said politely, "we'd like to speak to the Chief of Police. My name is Catherine McCorkle and this is Walter Sousa."

A blond policeman looked up at them curiously. "This is Sunday, Miss. The Chief always has Sunday breakfast with his family. He won't be by the office until later. Can I help you with something?"

"Well," Cookie said, looking over at Walter who nodded, "I guess we'd better talk to you then. We haven't much time." She glanced around to see that they were the only people in the room. Then she began telling the story of the McKenna Mansion and how strange things had been happening there.

"You see, I have a detective business and Walter here is my assistant. I'm sorry I don't have one of my cards with me, but I like to remain anonymous. It's better for business. Anyway, we think we've discovered a big, exotic bird-smuggling operation out of the McKenna Mansion."

The policeman smiled and put up his hand to stop her.

"Whoa, little missy. Are you sure you haven't been watching too much television?"

Before Cookie could answer, the other policeman got up from his desk and walked over to the reception counter.

"Let them talk, Jim. They may have something here. I heard on the radio the other day that a lot of endangered, rare birds were showing up along the coast. The FBI suspects some smuggling along here." He looked at Cookie.

"Go on, kid."

Cookie continued with her story about

how she and Walter went down the passage-way and discovered the room full of birds and what they heard Mark and the other man saying about moving the birds out tonight.

The second policeman turned to his partner. "Get the chief down here right away. I think the kid is telling the truth, and I think this is big!"

Cookie let out a sigh of relief and she and Walter went over to a bench and sat down to wait for the Chief. The policeman, whose name was Tony, came over and gave them a couple of candy bars he had gotten out of a machine. Cookie, who didn't much like candy, especially after cinnamon rolls, took the bar and put it in her pocket. Walter ate his immediately.

It wasn't long until the Chief came in through a back door. Cookie recognized him as the policeman who had come to tell Nancy about the fire at the McKenna house. He recognized her, too, and listened while she explained the story one more time. Afterward, Tony mentioned what he'd heard on the radio about the smuggling of birds in the area. The Chief nodded.

"I heard that, too, but it never occurred to me that it could be happening here in

Bluff Bay." He gestured to Tony. "Get that old work outfit out of the closet in back. I'm going back to the McKenna house with these kids. I'll act like a workman. We don't want to attract any attention until I've checked this out."

Cookie, Walter, and Moriarty rode toward the McKenna house in the Chief's wife's car.

"Now, I'm going to let you kids off here. I'll drive up and pretend I'm a workman; I've got a tool box. When you come in the house you can show me the passageway and the room with the birds."

Cookie told him the back door was open and she and Walter jumped out of the car a block from the McKenna house. When they reunited in the kitchen, Cookie and Walter took the Chief up to Mrs. McKenna's bedroom and opened the fireplace entrance with the crooked key. The Chief was flabbergasted when he saw the passageway.

"I'm going down and check things out," he said to Cookie and Walter. He pulled a flashlight from his tool box. "You kids stay here."

"I wanted to go down with him," Cookie grumbled as they sat on the bed and waited for the Chief to return.

"Not me," Walter said, scratching Moriarty's ears. "I'd rather be above ground anytime."

Twenty minutes later, Cookie and Walter heard the Chief coming up the ladder. He climbed into Mrs. McKenna's bedroom, closed the fireplace and turned the key. He shook his head in amazement.

"That's an incredible tunnel! You kids really discovered something. Old Captain McKenna was a pretty crafty man to set this up. It's a perfect smuggling arrangement. The trapdoor's way in the corner, and the building has been deserted for years. Only someone who was prowling around that old warehouse would have found the entrance. The property belongs to the city and there's been talk about what to do with it, but nothing has developed." He stuck the key in his pocket and turned to Cookie and Walter.

"Come on, I'll take you to Miss Merrit's house. After I talk to her about this, I'll go back to the office and phone the FBI. We'll stake out the place tonight."

"This is a big case, isn't it, Chief?" Cookie asked as they drove on to Nancy's house.

"It sure is, Catherine. You and Walter have done a good job."

Mrs. McCorkle's eyebrows rose when she saw Cookie and Walter at the door with a policeman. The Chief introduced himself with his rank and explained what he was doing with the children. Mrs. McCorkle only shook her head. She listened to his recounting of the story of the smuggling operation without saying a word.

"I should have known you two were up to something," she said finally.

"You should be very proud of these children," the Chief said. "This is not just a question of trespassing and smuggling. It's an important ecological issue. Conservationists will be very pleased if we stop these men."

"Well, at least you called in the police," Mrs. McCorkle said, looking at her daughter.

"Mother, I'm not foolish," Cookie said with indignation. She looked at Walter who stared back at her without expression. Cookie then turned to the Chief.

"Will you come over and tell us when you catch them? I won't be able to sleep well until I hear."

"If you don't mind being awakened, I'll come over personally," the Chief said. "Now I must get back to the station. We have a lot of planning to do."

"A secret passageway. I can't believe it," Nancy said, after the Chief had gone. "I always thought it was strange that there wasn't any basement in the house. Most houses of this era have basements. When the inspector came out to look at the foundation, they just checked around the perimeter of the house and said it was very solid. To think that all this time there has been smuggling going on. . . ." Her voice trailed off in amazement.

"What's even more astonishing is that I thought Cookie and Walter were relaxing up here," Mrs. McCorkle said.

"Well, I have to admit I didn't think I'd find a case," Cookie said. "Bluff Bay is pretty dead . . . ah, I mean quiet."

"Well, I'd like you children to stay inside the rest of the day," Mrs. McCorkle said. "I think I'll feel better if I know where you are every minute."

"I don't mind," Walter said. "I feel like taking it easy today."

"I'll read Sherlock Holmes to you," Cookie said and went in the bedroom to get her book.

The afternoon and evening went slowly for Cookie. When she wasn't reading to Walter, she was looking out the window restlessly. Walter, on the other hand, seemed perfectly comfortable lounging about the house. He was happy to go to bed early, although Cookie knew it would be hard for her to sleep. She dozed fitfully until she heard the front doorbell ring, then bounded out of bed and was the first one at the door. She opened it to find the Chief of Police and a tall man in a suit.

"We got 'em," the Chief said with a grin. "The two smugglers, all the birds, and the guy that was driving the truck."

Another Case Closed

"Were there more birds on the boat?" Cookie asked.

"Yes," the Chief replied. "At least two hundred. We have stopped a major smuggling ring." He paused and smiled. "Or I should say, you, young lady, and your assistant here have stopped a major smuggling ring."

By now, Walter, Mrs. McCorkle, and Nancy were standing at the door.

The Chief turned to the man next to him. "This is Agent Brady of the FBI. He wants to thank you, Catherine and Walter, for what you have done."

Agent Brady smiled at Cookie and Walter. "We are very grateful to you children. This has been a difficult case and we have had very few leads."

Cookie nodded and spoke in her most

grown-up voice. "Yes, Walter and I thought it was a difficult case, too. In fact, I think this case has had the fewest clues of any case we've worked on."

Looking over Cookie's head, Agent Brady cleared his throat and smiled at her mother.

"Well, I'm sure the television and press will want to interview you tomorrow and. . . ."

"No," Cookie interrupted. "We can't have our names known. We need to remain anonymous for future cases. Please just say two young detectives."

"I think that's best," Mrs. McCorkle murmured.

"Well . . . as you wish," Agent Brady responded.

"Anyway, thanks again, Catherine and Walter," the Chief said. "Oh, Miss Merrit, you should have that fireplace sealed. We are going to fill up the tunnel from the other side. We don't want this smuggling business to ever start up again."

"I'll have my workmen do that immediately—in the morning," Nancy said.

After the Chief and Agent Brady had gone, Cookie turned to go back to the bedroom.

"It would have been nice to be on television," Cookie said rather wistfully.

"Yes, but my mother would have developed a splitting headache," Walter said.

The following day, the newspapers in the area, the television and radio, were full of the news of the arrest of the smugglers, with pictures of Mark and his gang. To Nancy's surprise the phone at the McKenna Mansion rang non-stop with reservations. Everyone, it seemed, wanted to stay in a house with such an exciting history. Then, while the workmen were using cement to close up the fireplace, Cookie showed them all the secret compartment in the little table. Afterward, Walter suggested that Nancy bring it down into the library for her guests to see.

"You should display Mrs. McKenna's diary and the crooked key," he said. "People will go for it. It makes the house look like a museum."

"What a good idea!" Nancy exclaimed.

"Not bad thinking, Walter," Cookie said in appreciation. "If people are interested in staying here, they'll want to see as many parts of the smuggling operation as they can."

"I'll get a glass case for the diary and the key," Nancy said, her enthusiasm mounting. "And I can have a little brochure printed with the history of the house." She turned to Cookie.

"I'm so grateful to you and Walter, Cookie. Not only have you done a service to this community, solved a mystery about my house, but you've helped promote business."

Cookie smiled briefly, then she sighed. "If only we could have found out what really happened to Mrs. McKenna after the diary ended. That will always nag at me. Detectives don't like loose ends."

Just then the doorbell rang and Nancy went to answer it. Cookie could hear her talking to someone, then she watched Nancy usher a nice-looking older woman into the room.

"I'd like you all to meet Mrs. Frances Rydell. She's the librarian here in Bluff Bay." Nancy introduced everyone and they all shook hands politely.

"I wanted to come over and meet the children who solved the smuggling mystery," Mrs. Rydell said. "I know you want to be anonymous, but of course I know Nancy and I knew she was expecting a cousin and two children, so I put two and two together." She paused and took a piece of paper out of her purse. It looked like a letter, but it was yellowed and old.

"I also wanted to show you something. You see, my Aunt Mattie was a housemaid in the McKenna household when she was young. She left the job when Mrs. McKenna died and she never spoke about the house or the McKennas. When anyone ever asked her about the mysterious McKennas, she just said she didn't want to talk about them."

Mrs. Rydell took a deep breath and continued: "After I heard about the smuggling and the diary, my curiosity got the best of me and I went up into my attic to look through my Aunt Mattie's things. They'd been stored in one corner of the attic all those years . . . let me see, I think she died in 1925 because this letter is dated 1921. Anyway, I ran across this inside an old book of verse. I guess it had been overlooked when she died."

"What does it say?" Cookie asked. A surge of excitement ran through her. "Does it say anything about how Mrs. McKenna died?"

Mrs. Rydell nodded. "Yes, it does. I'd let you read it, but her handwriting is faint and hard to read, so I'll just tell you what it contains."

"Won't you sit down, Mrs. Rydell?" Nancy interrupted before Mrs. Rydell could tell them the contents of the letter. When everyone was seated, the woman continued. By now Cookie's heart was beating rapidly. Walter, too, was wide-eyed.

"Apparently, Aunt Mattie was coming to work one morning along a path in the side yard when she saw Mrs. McKenna lowering herself out of the bedroom window on a crude rope made up of bedclothes. Aunt Mattie was so surprised she couldn't move, but then seconds later Mrs. McKenna fell to the ground. It was a long fall, but she didn't make a sound. Aunt Mattie ran to her and saw immediately that she wasn't breathing. She ran into the house to get Captain McKenna and his sister. When they came back out, Captain McKenna said his wife was dead, that she had broken her neck. He then turned to Mattie and made her promise she would never tell anyone what happened that morning. The letter says that Captain McKenna looked at her with such fire in his eyes that Aunt Mattie was terrified and made him the promise. She was then dismissed from her job. Later that day she heard that there had been a fire in the McKenna house and that Mrs. McKenna had suffocated in the smoke. She knew this was not true, of course, but she said she could never reveal what really happened because she was afraid that Captain McKenna would come after her. Even when he boarded up the house and moved away, she didn't speak of Mrs. McKenna's death to anyone. She was afraid, too, that no one would believe her. As she says at the end of the letter, 'What would it matter? The poor woman was gone anyway.' I guess she wrote this letter at the end of her life just to get it off her conscience."

The library was silent for several minutes while everyone thought about poor Mrs. McKenna falling to her death from her bedroom window. Finally, Cookie spoke up.

"Thank you for telling us this, Mrs. Rydell. I am very sorry to hear about what really happened to Mrs. McKenna, but I'm glad the mystery of her death is solved. It bothered me, particularly after reading the diary and learning that she planned to try to get away from the McKenna Mansion."

"Maybe our knowing about it will make Mrs. McKenna's ghost rest now," Walter said.

Cookie frowned at him, but he just shrugged.

"Well, it does wind up the McKenna story," Nancy said.

"Would you like to have this letter, Cath-

erine?" Mrs. Rydell asked suddenly. "I think it should go to you because you did so much to clear up the mystery of the McKenna Mansion."

Cookie walked over to Mrs. Rydell. "I would be very happy to add it to the souvenirs from my cases, Mrs. Rydell. Thank you very much."

After Mrs. Rydell left and the group had gone back to Nancy's little rental house, Cookie studied the letter carefully. Mrs. Rydell was right. It was very hard to read. She folded it carefully and put it in an envelope Nancy had given her. It didn't matter if she could read it or not. She knew what it said and it was a great souvenir of a particularly tough case.

Walter came into the bedroom as Cookie was putting the letter in her suitcase.

"Your mother said we are going home in the morning. She said she's finished setting up Nancy's bookkeeping system and Nancy knows how to run her computer now."

"Well, then, I guess the cookies and milk came out even."

"What do you mean?" Walter asked.

"Oh, it's just an expression, Walter. In this case it means our timing is perfect. Nancy and Mom have finished their work and you and I have finished ours, both at the same time."

"Say, Cookie," Walter said slowly, "speaking of cookies. . . ." His voice trailed off and he grinned at her.

"What kind do you want, Walter?"

"How about something chewy?"

Cookie smiled. "I don't know why, but I thought you were going to say that. Do Granola Bars sound good to you?"

Walter chuckled. "Cookie, you must have been reading my mind."

Cookie McCorkle's Porcupine Meatballs

Serves 4

1 pound lean
  ground beef
¼ cup long-grain
  white rice
3 tablespoons
  minced onion
2 tablespoons
  minced fresh
  parsley
1 teaspoon
  dried leaf
  oregano

1 egg
½ teaspoon each
  salt and
  pepper
2 teaspoons oil
1 can (14-½ oz.)
  beef broth
¼ cup sour
  cream

1. In a mixing bowl, combine beef, rice, onion, parsley, oregano, crumbling the oregano between your fingers. Sprinkle in salt and pepper and break the egg on top.

2. With a large fork, stir all ingredients until they are well blended. (Do not mix this with your hands; Cookie is a firm believer that using your hands to mix meat tends to make it tough.)

3. Heat oil in 12-inch non-stick skillet and brown meatballs on all sides over a medium heat. These do not have to get too brown; it takes about 5 minutes.

4. Pour the beef broth over meatballs and heat until broth bubbles, then reduce heat and cover. Simmer for about 20 minutes, or until meatballs are no longer pink inside.

5. Remove pan from heat and carefully pour broth into a small bowl. Beat in sour cream so that the mixture is well blended, then pour it over the meatballs. Heat through and serve meatballs and sauce over rice or noodles, or serve with baked potatoes like Cookie does.

Cookie's Coleslaw

Serves 4

4 cups finely
   shredded
   cabbage
⅓ cup non-fat,
   unflavored
   yogurt
¼ cup
   mayonnaise

¼ cup
   buttermilk
2 tablespoons
   soy sauce
1 large clove
   garlic,
   pressed

1. Put cabbage in a bowl.

2. In a smaller bowl, combine yogurt with mayonnaise, buttermilk, soy sauce, and garlic. Mix well.

3. Fold dressing into cabbage and serve.

Cookie's Special North-Coast Chili

Serves 4

2 tablespoons
olive oil
⅔ cup chopped
onion
½ cup each
chopped
green
pepper,
chopped
celery
2 large cloves
garlic,
pressed
1½ teaspoons
chili powder

½ teaspoon
powdered
cumin
½ pound lean,
ground beef
1 can (16-oz.)
tomatoes
1 can (27-oz.)
kidney
beans, lightly
drained
salt, pepper

1. In a pot with a heavy bottom, heat oil and sauté onions with pepper and celery for 4 minutes over medium heat.

2. Stir in garlic, chili powder, cumin and beef and continue to cook over medium heat until beef is no longer pink.

3. Add tomatoes, breaking them up with a fork. Cover pot and reduce heat to simmer.

4. Cook for 20 minutes, then add kidney beans. Heat through and serve.

Cookie's Great Granola Bars

Makes 2 dozen bars

¾ cup melted butter or margarine

⅓ cup brown sugar

1 teaspoon vanilla

½ teaspoon salt

3 eggs

4 cups granola (homemade or commercial)

⅓ cup each shelled sunflower seeds and chopped walnuts (These can be eliminated if granola is full of nuts and sunflower seeds.)

1. In a mixing bowl, stir together butter and sugar, then add vanilla and salt. Beat in eggs until mixture is smooth.

2. Stir in granola, seeds, and nuts. Pack into a lightly buttered 9 × 13-inch baking dish.

3. Bake in preheated 350° oven for 23 to 25 minutes, or until lightly browned and firm. Cool and cut into squares.

Other Cookie McCorkle Books by
Sharon Cadwallader

COOKIE MCCORKLE AND THE
CASE OF THE KING'S GHOST

COOKIE MCCORKLE AND THE
CASE OF THE MISSING CASTLE

COOKIE MCCORKLE AND THE
CASE OF THE POLKA-DOT SAFECRACKER

Coming Soon

COOKIE MCCORKLE AND THE
CASE OF THE MYSTERY MAP

SHARON CADWALLADER lives in a small town
on the California coast. Her favorite pastimes are
writing mystery stories for children and cooking.